The Joke's on . . . Who?

At last Ms. Cheevy reached the door.

She pushed it open. She went inside.

There was a long moment of silence.

"Aaaaaaaahnnnnnnnnnnooooooooaaaaaahh!"

Ms. Cheevy screamed. She screamed more loudly than Bent had ever heard her scream. She screamed more loudly than Bent had ever heard anyone scream. She screamed more loudly than Bent thought was humanly possible. She screamed and screamed.

Then there was a crash. And silence.

Silence?

"Uh-oh," said Bent. But before he could say anything more, someone else began to scream. It sounded like a teakettle gone berserk.

"Eeeeeeeeeh!"

The door to Ms. Cheevy's classroom flew open. Polly stood in the doorway, her eyes wide in the red rim of makeup, her mouth a ghastly dark emptiness rimmed with red where Bent had painted her lips and blacked out her teeth.

"Eeeek! Euuuuuwwww! Sheeeee's dead!"

GRAVEYARD SCHOOL

Let's Scare the Teacher to Death!

Tom B. Stone

A SKYLARK BOOK

Toronto New York London Sydney Auckland

RL5.3,008–012

LET'S SCARE THE TEACHER TO DEATH!

A Skylark Book / September 1995

Skylark Books is a registered trademark of Bantam Books,
a division of Bantam Doubleday Dell Publishing Group, Inc.
Registered in U.S. Patent and Trademark Office and
elsewhere.

Graveyard School is a registered trademark of
Bantam Doubleday Dell Publishing Group, Inc.

ISBN 0-553-48337-4

Published simultaneously in the United States and Canada

Bantam Books are published by Bantam Books, a division of
Bantam Doubleday Dell Publishing Group, Inc. Its trademark,
consisting of the words "Bantam Books" and the portrayal of
a rooster, is registered in the U.S. Patent and Trademark Office
and in other countries. Marca Registrada. Bantam Books, 1540
Broadway, New York, New York 10036.

PRINTED IN THE UNITED STATES OF AMERICA

OPM   0 9 8 7 6 5 4 3 2 1

GRAVEYARD SCHOOL

Let's Scare the
Teacher to Death!

CHAPTER

1

Thump. Thump. Thump.

Silence.

"Shhh!" said Bent. "She's coming!"

The sixth-graders in Ms. Cheevy's second-period math class grew unnaturally quiet.

Bentley crouched lower behind the classroom door.

"Come on," he muttered.

Thump. Pause. *Thump.*

Bentley knew that the big, nervous, timid teacher sensed that something—or someone—was waiting for her. He knew she suspected that something bad was about to happen.

Was she hesitating with her hand on the doorknob? Looking over her shoulder for the help that wasn't coming? Wondering why she'd ever taken a job teaching at a place like Grove Hill School?

For a moment Bentley Jeste almost felt sorry for the terrified teacher. Almost.

1

Then he remembered who he was. And where he was.

Grove Hill Elementary School, also known as Graveyard School, was no place for pity.

He crouched lower.

The door handle turned. The door opened a fraction. A small brown eye peered over square, wire-rimmed glasses through the crack.

Everyone in the class instantly assumed an innocent expression and stared straight ahead at the blackboard.

Bent raised his arms over his head and made his hands into claws. He smiled a smile of gleeful anticipation.

In the back of the room, Jordie Flanders folded her arms and frowned. *Just do it,* she thought. *Just do it and get it over with.*

Jordie didn't feel sorry for Ms. Cheevy at all. In her opinion Ms. Cheevy was a great big coward. Worse, she was a terrible math teacher. The idea of one plus one seemed to confuse her. When Jordie, who was a mathhead, asked questions, Ms. Cheevy frowned and stared and swallowed nervously, her Adam's apple bobbing up and down out of sight behind her high-necked blouse. The answers she gave Jordie were often wrong.

This pitiful grasp of math in a math teacher meant, in Jordie's opinion, that Ms. Cheevy deserved whatever happened to her.

Just the same, Jordie never laughed at Bent's jokes, never participated in the big ones in which he enlisted other students in the class. But she didn't totally disapprove, either.

The brown eye disappeared from the crack in the door. The door shut again with a click.

The class held its collective breath.

Suddenly, without warning, Ms. Cheevy threw the door open hard.

It slammed back against the wall—or would have. But Bent, who'd been straightening up to leap out at Ms. Cheevy, stopped it.

The doorknob hit him right in the stomach. Hard.

"*Ooooh!*" he shouted instead of "Boo!", and staggered out from behind the door clutching his stomach.

Ms. Cheevy's eyes opened wide behind her glasses.

"*Aaaaah!*" she screamed. She screamed so loudly that the windowpanes rattled. A piece of chalk fell off the chalk tray at the blackboard. Screaming, she threw her arms up in the air, and the stack of papers she'd been carrying flew everywhere.

Bent reeled back to his desk through the storm of flying papers and fell into his seat. He clutched his stomach and tried to catch his breath.

Ms. Cheevy choked off her scream and stopped, looking wildly around.

Bentley gasped.

The rest of the class began to laugh. Chaos reigned.

Looking at Bentley's red, embarrassed face, Jordie began to laugh, too.

When class was over, Jordie walked over to Bent to gloat. "That was excellent, Bent. I've never laughed so hard in my life," she said.

At the front of the room Ms. Cheevy, twitching and muttering to herself, was erasing. Every time a locker slammed in the hall, she jumped as if she'd been shot. Class had just ended and the halls were full of students at their lockers, so the math teacher was hopping up and down like a rabbit.

A scared rabbit.

Bent got up from his seat. He'd been slumped over his desk, brooding. A simple jump-from-behind-the-door joke wasn't supposed to backfire like that. What had gone wrong?

He wished he could ignore Jordie's comment, but he couldn't. "Ha, ha," he said sarcastically. He didn't like Jordie very much.

"Good one, Bentman," Park Addams said, laughing. He gave Bent a friendly punch on the shoulder.

But Park, unlike Jordie, wasn't being sarcastic. Park, along with most of the kids in the class, was one of Bent's admirers, one of the people who described Bent as "wired to the weird" in admiring tones.

"She really jumped, didn't she?" said Bent, feeling slightly better.

"To the sky. But the best part was when she slammed the door open in Bent's stomach," said Jordie in a loud voice. "Didn't you think so?"

Bent's stomach gave a twinge. He began to walk quickly out of the classroom.

At the front of the room, Ms. Cheevy sat down at her desk, pushing her chair back so that it pressed against

4

the wall. She put her hand on her desk drawer handle and stopped. She frowned.

This was not surprising, since things had leaped out of her desk drawers at her more than once.

As Bentley watched, she jerked the drawer open. She flinched. But nothing jumped out.

Ms. Cheevy looked up. Her eyes met Bent's. For a moment they seemed to blaze in a very unrabbitlike way.

Bent blinked in surprise.

Quickly Ms. Cheevy lowered her eyes to the contents of the drawer and began to rummage around inside.

Bent shook his head. He was imagining things. He hoped he wasn't developing a guilty conscience.

How did Ms. Cheevy get to be such a coward? he wondered as he left the classroom. *It couldn't just be from teaching at Graveyard School.*

Could it?

Bent paused outside the girls' bathroom on the first floor. He sighed. It had such potential for a perfect practical joke. But what? A smoke bomb released at a strategic moment? A mouse or a snake?

"You know, Bentley, someday you're going to go too far," said a disapproving voice.

Bent spun around, then relaxed. It was only prissy Polly Hannah, the biggest pain in the whole school.

"I thought you weren't speaking to me," he said. Polly had *not* laughed when Bentley had put the whoopee cushion in her chair at the most recent school assembly.

5

But then, what had he expected? She never laughed at the whoopee-cushion joke. Some people had no sense of humor.

"It's childish not to speak to someone," said Polly in her prim, shrill voice. "And *I'm* not childish. You are."

Bent was sorry she *had* started speaking to him again. He decided not to get into it with her. After all, who had said "One joke is worth a thousand words"?

Oh yes. He himself had said that. And then there was his mother's favorite: "Actions speak louder than words." How true.

He wouldn't dignify Polly's pathetic insult with a reply. He would let his actions speak for him. Soon. Very soon.

He started to turn away, dwelling on the lovely vision of himself releasing a snake in the bathroom just after Polly had gone inside. Her blond curls would stand on end. Her pale blue eyes would pop out of her head.

Just then Maria Medina came up. She put her hand on the bathroom door, then stopped and gave Bent a suspicious look. "What are you doing hanging around *here*?" she demanded.

"I'm not," Bent said quickly.

"I told Bent that one day he was going to go too far," said Polly.

"Why don't you go take a long walk off a short diving board," said Bent to Polly.

"She's telling the truth," said Maria. "One day Dr. Morthouse is going to catch you at it, Bent, instead of just Mr. Lucre, and then—"

"Huh. Dr. Morthouse. Big deal. I'm not afraid of her."

"You should be," said Maria.

Dr. Morthouse was the principal of the school and one reason that the school's nickname fit so well. People feared Dr. Morthouse. No one was quite sure why. She always spoke softly. She often smiled.

Maybe it was the flash of silver that sometimes glinted in her mouth when she bared her teeth. Many people believed the silver glint came from a fang.

But it could have just been the way she smiled—like a lion about to enjoy dinner.

The assistant principal, Mr. Lucre, was another matter. He was a man who oozed through life, rubbing sweaty palms together and believing that no one noticed the bald spot shining on the top of his head beneath the three strands of limp brown hair that he kept greased across the top. Mr. Lucre's smile, especially when he licked his lips and said, "Remember, kids, the principal is your *pal*," was disgusting.

But not terrifying.

Bent put the thought of Dr. Morthouse's terrifying fang-filled smile out of his head and said, "Well, I'm not afraid of her. Dr. Morthouse isn't so tough. Even if she did catch me, it wouldn't matter."

Suddenly Maria said in a strangled voice, "Bent."

Polly's cheeks turned pink. Her mouth opened.

"That surprises you?" Bent said. "You think I'm like Ms. Cheevy? You think I'm like the rest of the wimps in this school?"

Polly's lips moved.

Maria said, "Ah, Bent, ah . . ."

"Ha." Bent was really on a roll now. "She's big, she's mean, but so what? I laugh at danger." He flung his arm out. "I—"

His arm hit something large and unyielding.

Polly's cheeks went from pink to pale. Maria took a little step back.

The hair on Bent's neck stood up.

He turned, fearing the worst.

Dr. Morthouse, her arms crossed, a little smile on her face, was standing right behind him.

CHAPTER
2

"Aaaaah!" said Bent, jumping back and crashing into Maria.

"Hello, Bentley," Dr. Morthouse answered. "I'm *so* sorry. I didn't mean to startle you. It's so rude when someone does that, don't you agree?"

Polly gave a little gasp. "She knows," she whispered.

"Know? What is it I know, Polly?" Dr. Morthouse switched her steely gaze from Bentley to Polly.

Bent and Maria both turned to glare at Polly, Bent because he didn't want Polly telling the principal about his attempt to leap out from behind the classroom door to scare Ms. Cheevy, Maria because no matter how rotten Bent's jokes were, it was even more rotten to tell on a kid to a teacher. Or a principal.

Polly opened her mouth. She looked at Maria. She closed her mouth again. Then she opened it.

She looked like a fish.

"Well?" prompted Dr. Morthouse.

"About, about good manners. You know about good manners," said Maria, heading Polly off. "We were just talking about how rude some people can be."

Maria grabbed Polly's arms and yanked her toward the bathroom door. "Ah, we've got to hurry to, uh, you know. I mean, it's almost time for the next class."

Without waiting for Dr. Morthouse to reply, Maria ducked into the bathroom.

"Hey—" Bent heard Polly say in protest. Then the bathroom door whooshed shut.

"Well?" repeated Dr. Morthouse.

Bent opened his own mouth. No sound came out. How did Dr. Morthouse do that? He was saved by a yell. It came from the boys' bathroom at the end of the hall. It was followed by another. There was definitely a fight going on down there.

Dr. Morthouse's eyes narrowed. For one moment she kept her gaze fastened on Bent. Bent tried to look innocent. He wished he could turn invisible.

Then Dr. Morthouse swung around and marched down the hall. Reaching the boys' bathroom, she pushed the door wide and said in a low, threatening, carrying voice, "This is Dr. Morthouse. What is going on in there?"

Whoever it was broke off in midyell.

"Nothing," someone croaked in a panicked voice. A voice full of guilt.

"Very well," said Dr. Morthouse. "In that case, you won't mind my coming in on the count of three.

"One . . . two . . ."

It was too horrible to watch.   Bent turned and ran.

Jordie slammed her math book shut in disgust. "I don't believe this," she muttered.

Ms. Cheevy had been so rattled by Bent that she'd given them the same homework assignment she'd given them the week before.

So rattled—or so indifferent to what she was teaching.

Jordie sighed. She realized that if she called up her friends Maria Medina or Stacey Carter to complain, they'd think she was out of her mind. All the other kids in the class were probably delighted not to have math homework that night.

Opening the book again, Jordie skipped ahead a couple of chapters. She worked until a shadow fell across her desk.

"Hi, Mom," she said, without looking up. "How was your day?"

Her mother kissed the top of her head before Jordie had time to duck. "Fine. How was yours, dear?"

"Mathematically deficient," said Jordie.

Mrs. Flanders glanced at the sheet of paper on Jordie's desk. "It doesn't look as if you're suffering from any lack of geometry to me," she said. "In fact, it looks to me as if you could use a break."

"Aw, Mom. You're not going to give me that speech about—"

"Indeed I am. Go outside. Get some fresh air and exercise. Play with your friends."

"Play," Jordie said with withering scorn.

"Play," Mrs. Flanders said firmly.

Jordie slammed her book shut a second time and jumped to her feet. "Most parents would be glad to have a kid who did all her homework and liked to study."

"Play," said Mrs. Flanders. "Have fun. Okay?"

"Puh-lease," said Jordie as she stomped out of the house.

The afternoon newspaper almost took off the top of her head.

"Hey!" she shouted.

The kid on the bicycle slowed to a stop, the next newspaper already in his hand. "Sorry!" he said.

Jordie recognized Algie Green, who was sort of new at Graveyard School.

"S'all right," she said.

Algie grinned. "If you were Bent, you'd have pretended I knocked you out or something."

"Bent is a childish, immature brat," Jordie said heatedly.

Algie looked surprised at Jordie's vehemence. "His jokes get kind of old," Algie said. "But some of them are funny." He thought for a moment, then said, "But I bet Ms. Cheevy hates it. I know I hated it when I first got to Graveyard School and Jason Dunnbar kept picking on me."

"Yeah, but you fought back," said Jordie.

"I guess," said Algie. "But I sort of had help."

Jordie knew that Algie was referring to the headless bicycle rider he was said to have encountered on his paper route. No one knew what the whole story was, or exactly how Jason was involved. They only knew that Jason no longer seemed to have it in for Algie, while Algie seemed content to stay out of Jason's way.

It was something that neither of them ever talked about—just another of the many weird things, besides the old graveyard on the hill above the elementary school, which gave Graveyard School its nickname.

"I wonder why Ms. Cheevy doesn't do something," said Algie. "I mean, she's so tall and everything."

"She's a big chicken," said Jordie.

Algie said, "Are you in a bad mood or something?"

Jordie shrugged. "She is a big chicken. A big, strange chicken," she said more mildly. "And a terrible math teacher."

"There are worse teachers at school," Algie said. He'd started walking his bicycle along. Now he threw a newspaper against the door of a house with a solid thump.

"True," said Jordie. "Nice shot, by the way."

"Thanks. I use my paper route to practice for baseball."

"A very interesting game, statistically speaking," said Jordie. "I mean, look at the designated hitter rule. What, mathematically speaking, has that done to the batting averages of the American League? Have you ever thought about it?"

Pushing his glasses up onto the bridge of his nose and looking slightly alarmed, Algie said, "Ah, not exactly like that. But it sounds, ah, interesting. Well, gotta go. See ya later." He hopped on his bicycle and rode away.

Jordie stifled a sigh. She was just going to have to accept the fact that other people didn't find numbers as fascinating as she did. *Maybe Mom's right. I'm going to have a long and boring childhood*, she thought, *if I'm not careful.*

She'd turned and headed back down the sidewalk toward her house. Maybe she'd go up to the park and see if Stacey was up there. Like Algie, Stacey worked to earn extra money, but she didn't deliver papers. She walked dogs and fed cats and watered plants for people while they were on vacation. When she wasn't walking other people's dogs in the park, she often hung out there with her own dog, Morris, and sometimes with her best friend, Maria.

Maybe I could get a job, thought Jordie.

She was thinking so hard that she didn't hear the screaming until the bicycle was almost on top of her.

"Look out! Look out! The brakes are go-o-o-o-ne!"

CHAPTER
3

Jordie looked over her shoulder.

A kid on a bicycle was shooting down the sidewalk toward her. The front wheel of the bicycle was wobbling dangerously out of control.

As Jordie leaped to one side, she realized that she recognized the kid on the bicycle.

"Ow!" screamed Jordie. *"My ankle!"*

She fell.

The bicycle was almost on top of her.

She threw up her hands. *"Stop!"* she screamed. *"Help!"*

Bent straightened up suddenly and wrenched the bicycle to one side, slamming on the brakes.

He fell off in a heap on the grass. The bike fell on top of him.

For the second time that day, Jordan Flanders began to laugh at Bentley Jeste.

"Gotcha!" she said.

Gasping, Bentley sat up. "What do you mean?" he said.

"My ankle isn't hurt, see?" Jordie held up one foot. "I figured it was just one of your dumb jokes."

Bentley's face turned very red. "Dumb jokes. *Dumb jokes!* Are you crazy? You could have killed me!"

Jordie sat up. She hated to admit it, but she'd actually enjoyed pulling that stupid stunt on Bent.

"You could've killed me, too," she pointed out calmly.

Bent Jeste, prankman, stared at Jordie Flanders, mathhead, in shock.

The shock of recognition.

Was it possible that he had at long last met his match?

Jordie folded her arms, a gleam in her eye. "Admit it," she said. "It was a good one, Bentley. You just wish you'd thought of it."

Bentley jumped up and grabbed the bicycle. He got on it without saying a word and pedaled furiously away.

Jordie got up, too. She watched him ride into the sunset.

That had been fun. Multiples of fun. Fun to the *x* power.

Go out and play, her mother had said. *Go out and have some fun.*

Maybe her mother hadn't meant go out and turn into a joke monster.

But Jordie wasn't about to ask questions.

She just wanted to have more fun.

*   *   *

No one was on the steps of the old stone school building when Bentley arrived early the next morning.

"Are you sure you'll be all right?" his father said. Mr. Jeste was on his way to a breakfast business meeting. Bentley had seen a chance to get to school before anyone else. With an early start, the possibilities for practical jokes were endless.

"I'll be fine," he told his father. "Don't worry about me."

Mr. Jeste stared at his oldest son for a long moment. Then he said, "I'm not. It's the rest of the world I worry about."

Bent knew better than to say "Trust me." He just made a face and tried to look relatively innocent.

He didn't think he succeeded very well. His father glanced at his watch, glanced at the school, then shook his head and sighed. He looked over his shoulder several times before he drove away.

Bentley waved.

Innocently.

The moment his father was out of sight, he took off.

The school was still dark inside. Dark and quiet. Keeping his eyes open for Dr. Morthouse or—maybe even worse—Basement Bart, the strange school caretaker, Bent sped down the halls to Ms. Cheevy's room.

He liked the dark and the quiet. *I ought to get to school early more often,* he thought.

The door was unlocked. He pushed it open slowly and peered cautiously around it. Not that he expected to find

17

Ms. Cheevy inside. She was usually one of the last teachers to arrive at the school. And the first to leave.

Her heart clearly wasn't in her work.

He stepped inside the classroom.

And a voice said softly in his ear, "What are you doing here?"

He leaped straight into the air.

He almost screamed.

He came down swinging. Jordie just managed to get out of his way.

When he'd regained his wits, Bent snarled, "What am *I* doing here? What are *you* doing here?"

"I asked you first," said Jordie in her superior tone.

Bent glared at her. She glared at him.

Jordie broke first. She wasn't used to living so dangerously.

"Math homework," she said. "I was doing math homework."

What a math nerd, Bentley thought contemptuously.

Then he remembered that they had no math homework. He smiled his most menacing smile. "Oh yeah? Math homework? I don't think so," he said with a sneer.

Jordie felt her face flush. If she was going to pursue the lower things in life, she was going to have to learn to think faster. She said, "So who cares what you think?"

They faced each other like two dogs, ready for a fight.

Something squeaked and rattled in the hall.

"Basement Bart! Quick! Hide!" Bent dove for the teacher's desk. Behind him, Jordie froze.

The sound of Bart's cleaning wagon stopped outside the classroom door.

Jordie watched, her eyes wide, as the door began to open. She was about to get caught by Basement Bart in the school before hours. *Why*, she wondered desperately, *did he have to stop and check on Ms. Cheevy's classroom? Why this classroom out of all the other classrooms?*

She felt her knees go weak. Basement Bart's big, hulking shadow fell across the threshold as the door opened. His hand reached inside the door to flick the light switch. It was big and hairy. It looked like a werewolf's paw.

Then she was yanked backward so hard that her feet practically left the floor. The next thing she knew, she was crammed up under Ms. Cheevy's old wooden desk with Bent.

Basement Bart walked slowly into the classroom, grumbling under his breath. He lifted up the trash can beside the desk. He dropped it. He clumped slowly around the room, stopping from time to time.

What is he doing? Jordie wondered.

Finally, after what seemed like forever, he said, "Hmmmph," and turned and walked out of the room.

Bent backed out from under the desk and straightened up.

The door opened again.

Jordie, kneeling at the edge of the desk, watched in

horror. She heard Bent take a short, sharp breath above her.

Basement Bart's big, hairy hand slid inside the door and turned the light out. The door closed again with a thump.

They stayed frozen for another full minute. Then Bent let out a long, slow breath. "That was a close one," he said.

"Too close," muttered Jordie. Maybe she wasn't cut out for this life after all. Then she said to Bent, only half-grudgingly, "Thanks. You saved my life."

Bent looked embarrassed. "Nah. He wouldn't have killed you. Besides, how did I know you wouldn't rat me out?"

Indignantly Jordie said, "I'd never do that, no matter what."

"You wouldn't?"

"No way!" All her animosity toward Bent returned. "How could you say such a stupid, rotten, dumb thing?"

"Sorry," said Bent. "It's just that—"

"What?" she snapped.

"Well, I don't know. It's just that, you know, you're such a teacher's pet and all."

"I am not!"

Bent opened his mouth. He closed it again. Then he said, "Well, you are, you know."

"Getting the answers right doesn't mean I'm a teacher's pet. Neither does getting good grades. I make straight one hundreds on Cheevy's tests and I'm not her pet.''

"True," said Bent. He looked around the room. "Cheevy," he said, suddenly remembering where he was and why he'd come. He looked back at Jordie and a blinding light went off in his brain. "Cheevy!" he repeated. "You don't like Cheevy at all, do you? You're always giving her math whacks.''

"She deserves them. She shouldn't even be teaching," said Jordie. "She doesn't know a fraction from a fracture,''

"Then it's true," said Bent.

"What?''

Bent smiled. "You came here to pull one on Cheevy, didn't you? Just like I did!''

CHAPTER

4

"This," said Ms. Cheevy, "is a point." She drew a white dot on the blackboard. The chalk squeaked. She winced. "A point is the end of a line."

Jordie's hand shot up. "Ms. Cheevy? Excuse me, Ms. Cheevy?"

Ms. Cheevy turned slowly, reluctantly. She was in her usual high-necked outfit: a blouse buttoned up to the chin that barely concealed her nervously bobbing Adam's apple, a baggy, high-collared blue jacket, a long navy-blue skirt that stopped just above her ankles, and large, flat navy-blue shoes. The only bright color came from thick, pale blue tights. The stockings Ms. Cheevy wore were her fashion statements: Lots and lots of different kinds of tights in all kinds of stripes and patterns and colors.

But she did *not* look like a model in them.

"Ms. Cheevy?"

"Yes, Jordie," said Ms. Cheevy at last, peering out over her glasses.

"How do you know?"

"Know what?" said Ms. Cheevy, sounding almost annoyed.

"Know that a point is the end of a line? I mean, can you see it? Is it just a flat dot?"

With a sigh Ms. Cheevy said, "Because that's what it is." She held her chalk up and quoted, " 'A point is the end of a line.' "

"It's not in our book," said Jordie.

That stopped Ms. Cheevy. She paused. "It's not?"

Jordie folded her arms and shook her head. Out of the corner of her eye, she saw Bent lean slightly forward over his desk.

"Well, it's true, just the same," said Ms. Cheevy. "But since it's not in the book, never mind."

Polly fluttered her fingers. "Does that mean we don't have to know it for a test?"

At that exact moment, Bentley's desk tipped over. He gave a horrible cry as he fell. His head smashed against the floor and he lay still.

Everyone froze. Then Polly looked down. Her eyes widened. "Blood!" she screamed. "It's *blood!*"

Jordie rushed forward. As she reached Bentley, her foot slipped in the red pool that haloed his head. She went straight up in the air and fell heavily.

Her head rolled limply to one side. Blood began to run out of her mouth.

Polly screamed more and more loudly. "Eeek! Eeek! Eeek!"

"Oh no!" cried Ms. Cheevy. "I'll go—no . . . someone . . . Maria, go for help! Stand back, everybody!"

She rushed toward the two fallen students and then
stopped as waves of laughter erupted around the room.

Jordie sat up and wiped the sticky ketchup from the
corner of her mouth. Bentley scrambled to his feet and
peeled up the red plastic gag pool of blood from the floor.

Polly stopped screaming.

"I can't believe you fell for that," Bent said to Polly.

Polly's face turned redder than usual.

Jordie and Bent exchanged high fives. Only then did
Jordie look over at Ms. Cheevy.

She was standing stock-still in the middle of the room,
her hand at her throat, her eyes huge behind her glasses.

"You're going to *get* it, both of you," Polly whispered
viciously.

Park was doubled over, laughing. "G-Good one," he
gasped. "Even better than the time Jaws pretended he'd
been poisoned in the lunchroom."

"Thank you," Bentley said modestly. "But I couldn't
have done it without Jordie's help."

"Jordie?" said Maria, puzzled. "Jordie! You?"

Jordie didn't answer. She stared at Ms. Cheevy, who
was walking slowly, rigidly toward the front of the room.
Something about that stiff and stately walk unnerved her.
Had they gone too far? Was Ms. Cheevy about to break
down? Or worse, send them to the principal's office?

Ms. Cheevy turned. Her face was a frozen mask. She
didn't speak.

The room got quiet.

Quieter than it had ever been the whole time Ms. Cheevy had been a teacher.

Without blinking, Ms. Cheevy stared at her students. Her gaze wandered over the room. For a moment it stopped on Jordie.

And for a moment Jordie was almost sorry for what she'd done, sorry that she'd helped Bent out. Then she remembered the thrill of the moment, pulling the gag, watching everyone gasp, and listening to Polly's shrill scream.

No. No, it had been worth it. It had definitely been worth it.

It had been *fun,* no matter what happened.

Ms. Cheevy smiled. "How . . . interesting," she said. "Well. What a creative class you are. If only you were as creative about getting your homework done."

She looked down at the papers on her desk. She looked back up. She smiled again. "Put your books away. Take out one sheet of paper and a pencil."

"We're not going to have a test, are we?" said Park.

Ms. Cheevy smiled. "That's exactly what we're going to have. A nice test." Her eyes went from Park to Bent to Jordie. Something sparkled in them, behind her glasses, a crazy gleam, a nasty glint. "And let me assure you, students, that this test will be no joke."

"That was *all* your fault, Bentley," Polly said furiously as they walked out into the hall. "I can't believe you made her do that."

Bentley didn't answer. He was limp with shock. That hadn't been a simple pop quiz that Cheevy the Timid had just given the class—that had been the Evil Exam to End All Exams.

He was lucky if he'd gotten even one answer right.

To Bent's surprise, Jordie said, "It's not all Bent's fault, you know. I helped."

Maria said, "Why did you do that, Jordie? Not that it matters. Everybody knows how good at math you are. You probably aced the test."

But Jordie was in as much shock as Bent and the rest of the class. For the first time in her life, the numbers had let her down. She was very much afraid that she hadn't aced the test. Worse, she was afraid she might even have made a B on it.

Realizing that talking about this last fear would not endear her to her fellow students, she merely shook her head. "I didn't know the answers," she said. "She got me, too."

Looking back, Park said, "She's standing there, watching us. Look at her."

They all looked back over their shoulders. Sure enough, Ms. Cheevy was framed by the doorway to her classroom. She had her arms folded. For once she wasn't slumping forward in her big, loose, oversized clothes. She looked, for Ms. Cheevy, pleased. Even proud.

And for once she didn't look scared at all.

When she saw them looking in her direction, she straightened up even more. Then she gave them all a big, mean grin. A very un-Cheevy-like grin. A first-class weird and nasty Graveyard School smile.

The old school smile, thought Bentley, his brain refusing to take it all in. *What's come over Cheevy the worm, Cheevy the rabbit?*

They all turned back around quickly.

"I don't like this," said Park.

"Me either," said Maria. "Did you see the look on her face? She hates us."

"Aw, she'll forget it by tomorrow," argued Bentley. But his voice lacked conviction.

"Well, if she doesn't. . . ." Polly let her voice trail off threateningly before turning to march down the hall with her nose in the air.

"She won't," Jordie said softly.

The image of Cheevy standing triumphantly in the doorway of her classroom was imprinted in Jordie's brain.

Was it possible for Ms. Cheevy to change so completely, so suddenly? To go from terrified to terrible?

It was like a math problem with some pieces missing. A problem without an answer.

Or worse, an answer that Jordie wasn't interested in finding out.

She looked quickly over her shoulder one more time. Ms. Cheevy hadn't moved.

"Come *on,*" ordered Jordie, and grabbed Maria's arm.

Suddenly Ms. Cheevy, standing all alone in the doorway, looked very big. Very bad. Very dangerous.

Suddenly Jordie was afraid.

CHAPTER
5

The next day Dr. Morthouse stood in the front door of the school, surveying her subjects. As usual, they were huddled according to age, the little kids on the lowest steps, the older kids at the top.

"Another great day for preparing little minds for the future," said Dr. Morthouse.

Her assistant principal, Hannibal Lucre, rubbed his plump hands together. He licked his lips and smiled nervously. Was the boss making a joke? Should he laugh, or solemnly agree?

Just then Ms. Cheevy came up the front steps. She pushed through the students as if she didn't even see them. The younger students reacted to her as they did to all teachers: They got out of her way.

The older students moved more reluctantly, more slowly. A few of them gave Ms. Cheevy dark, angry glances.

Ms. Cheevy marched on, looking neither left nor right.

Dr. Morthouse thought, *Something's wrong.* Her principal's radar went on full alert.

"Ms. Cheevy," said Mr. Lucre as the math teacher came through the front door. "Another great day for preparing little minds for the future, eh?"

Ms. Cheevy looked down at the plump vice-principal. "What are you talking about?" she demanded.

Startled by the meek teacher's brusque tone, Mr. Lucre flushed. "Well, er . . . you know."

"No, I don't know!" she snapped. She prepared to push by them.

Clearly Ms. Cheevy was not in a good mood.

Reaching out, Dr. Morthouse caught the teacher's sleeve. Ms. Cheevy stopped and looked down at Dr. Morthouse. Dr. Morthouse was an imposing person, but she wasn't as large as Ms. Cheevy.

"What is it?" said Ms. Cheevy. To Mr. Lucre's horror, the math teacher's tone was only slightly less brusque when talking to the principal. Unconsciously he wrung his hands. "Oh dear, oh dear!" he moaned softly.

Neither of them noticed him. Dr. Morthouse had to look up to meet Ms. Cheevy's eyes; Ms. Cheevy didn't look away. The two of them stared at each other.

Then Dr. Morthouse said, "Is there some kind of problem, Cheevy?"

"No," said Ms. Cheevy. She glanced left and right, checked over her shoulder and over Dr. Morthouse's. "No," she repeated, more hoarsely.

"No?" said Dr. Morthouse.

Ms. Cheevy looked back over her shoulder. The first bell hadn't rung yet, but students had begun to press against the door. Through the glass paneling she could see faces. Familiar faces. Faces she'd come to know.

And to fear.

The faces of her second-period math students.

Why had she chosen this career? She'd never meant to be a teacher. Anything was better than this.

Anything.

She looked back into Dr. Morthouse's hard gray eyes. Better not to let the principal know. Better to keep quiet. If she could just last for a while longer, she could retire.

Unless her class drove her to early retirement—the permanent, horizontal kind. The grim thought almost made her smile.

She realized Dr. Morthouse was still watching her intently.

"Nothing I can't handle," she finally said. She left before Dr. Morthouse could ask any more questions, but not before Mr. Lucre had started up again. She heard his plaintive voice all the way down the hall until she turned the corner: "Oh dear, oh dear, oh dear."

"Maybe Dr. Morthouse fired her," said Maria.

"In your dreams," said Polly, sticking her nose in the air.

"I can see up your nose," said Bent.

Maria and Stacey snickered. So did Jordie, who had just come up the steps.

"You are *so* gross, Bentley," Polly answered. "I hate you."

"That scares me," said Bent. But his mind wasn't really on his words. He was thinking about Ms. Cheevy.

Something about the way she'd walked up the stairs into the school worried him. And what had Dr. Morthouse said to her? Worse, what had she said to Dr. Morthouse? Had she reported him at last?

No. No, because Dr. Morthouse would have marched out onto the steps and seized Bent. Of that he was sure.

Then why had Dr. Morthouse looked so grim when Ms. Cheevy disappeared down the hall?

The bell rang.

"Another day, another joke, right, Bent One?" asked Park, bounding up the stairs.

"Right, man," said Bent.

"Excellent!" said Park enthusiastically.

"Failed? I failed a math *quiz*?" Jordie's voice went into opera diva range. "This is not possible."

"I didn't pass, either," said Polly in a tone of stunned disbelief.

Bent forgot his own troubles, spelled with a big fat F— on the top of his math quiz, to look up at Polly and sneer. "Poor Polly. See where being good will get you?"

Dismissing Polly's failure, and everyone else's, as irrelevant, Jordie bounded to her feet. "Ms. Cheevy!"

Ms. Cheevy, who was handing out the pop quiz papers

to the last row of students, jumped. She gasped. Then she said in a low, hoarse voice, "Yes?"

"There's a mistake here," said Jordie. "On my test."

Ms. Cheevy raised her eyebrows. "A mistake."

"A big mistake," said Jordie firmly.

"I'll be going over the tests in just a moment, Jordie."

"But—"

"Sit down!" The order rapped out so suddenly and so unexpectedly that Jordie sat down with her mouth still open.

"Aliens have taken over Ms. Cheevy," muttered Bent. Park snorted.

Ms. Cheevy's head came up like a dog catching a scent in the wind. "Did you have something you wanted to share with the class, Bentley? Parker?"

"No ma'am," Park said quickly.

"No," said Bent.

An uneasy hush fell over the class as its tall, formerly terrified teacher handed out the last test and went back to her desk. As she turned to face her students, a car backfired outside in the parking lot.

Ms. Cheevy jumped. Her face turned pale. She staggered a little and her hand flew to her heart. With her other hand, she grabbed the edge of the desk so hard that her knuckles turned white.

Bent watched her like a hawk.

Although Bent didn't realize it, Jordie was doing the same thing.

They were both waiting, hoping that Ms. Cheevy would break. Become her timid old self again.

But at the last minute, by an enormous act of will, Ms. Cheevy regained control of herself. Although perspiration broke out along her upper lip, she managed not to shriek or shrink.

She took a deep breath. She narrowed her eyes. "Now, class," she said, "shall we go over our tests?"

"You let them give you the mystery meat?" asked Park.

Bentley looked down at his tray. He'd been too disheartened to even make gross food jokes. And although he had a very lifelike rubber cockroach in his pocket, one he carried especially for food occasions, he didn't feel like using it.

He was, for the first time in his life, in the grip of guilt. It was an ugly feeling.

He felt guilty for what he'd done to Ms. Cheevy. He'd pushed her over the edge. He'd gone too far.

He'd turned Ms. Cheevy into the Math Teacher from the Dark Side.

He resolved to suffer his guilt in silence. He didn't want the rest of the class on his case. That would just make it worse.

He followed Park to the table of guys sitting in the corner of the lunchroom. Jaws was at one end, forking food into his mouth without seeming to chew.

"Meatloaf!" said Jaws joyously.

"Roadkill," corrected Park.

Jaws shrugged and kept chewing. "Same dif," he mumbled.

Bent put his tray down, stared at his plate for a moment, then picked it up and pushed it over to Jaws.

"Thanks," said Jaws.

Algie slid into the seat across from Bent.

"Tough times at Graveyard School," Algie offered. "I heard about that math test. Bad news, man."

"It totaled me," Park said sadly. "I just hope my mom doesn't find out. This could seriously affect my baseball practice time."

"Is Ms. Cheevy doing this to other classes?" Bent asked. He hoped he sounded merely curious. Not guilty.

"Nope," said Algie. He paused. "Although she has been acting a little strange the last couple of days."

"Like how?" asked Park.

"Like jumpy. But fighting it, you know? And every once in a while, she sort of loses it like a normal teacher does, and lets us have it."

"Like discipline?" Bent asked.

Algie thought for a moment. "No. Worse. Like mean. Like her eyes squinch up and her voice gets all hoarse and she looks . . . bigger."

"Aliens," Bent said. "She's being taken over by aliens."

"Bentman, I've got bad news for you. That only happens in books," said Park.

Jaws nodded vigorously to show he was still in the conversation. He swallowed. "Maybe she's turned over a new leaf. You know, like when my parents go on one of their new diets."

Jaws's parents were health-food fanatics who often tried to pressure Jaws into living on strange and horrifying food—food, according to Jaws, even more horrifying than roadkill. Their new diets also often included new exercise programs, new exercise equipment, and new exercise clothes.

"Maybe it's something she ate," Jaws went on.

"That is the dumbest thing I ever heard in my life," said Polly from the next table.

"Who asked you?" snapped Bent.

"She's not acting like this because of something she ate," said Polly relentlessly. "She's acting like this because of something that happened."

Bentley knew what was coming. He saw Maria and Stacey put down their forks. He realized that at his table even Jaws had stopped in midbite.

"What? What happened to Ms. Cheevy?" asked Maria.

Polly pointed at Bent, her cheeks pink with triumph. "Bentley!" she said. "Bentley is what happened. It was his dumb practical joke that made Ms. Cheevy go crazy. It's Bentley and Jordie's fault!"

"Now *that's* the dumbest thing I ever heard!" said Bent. He laughed loudly.

Guiltily.

He laughed alone.

All the girls at the next table were staring at him. All the guys at his table were, too.

Then, to his horror, Jordie nodded slowly. "Although I don't think much of your powers of reasoning, Polly, what you've said makes a kind of sense."

Polly smiled. Then frowned. "Wait a minute," she said, struggling to decide whether Jordie was insulting her or complimenting her.

"Hey!" yelped Bent. "Whose side are you on, anyway?"

"Don't be silly, Bent," said Jordie, her voice detached and cool. "It's not a matter of sides. We have a problem here and we have to solve it."

"Well, I blame Bentley. I think it's all his fault," said Polly.

"You always think everything is someone else's fault," said Maria under her breath.

Jordie held up her hand. "We're wasting time here. I believe that Polly's theory is, in fact, correct. A basic case of what equals x."

"What did you just say?" Jaws asked with his mouth full once again.

"She said it's as simple as one plus one equals two," said Algie.

"Not exactly," said Jordie, "but that's not important now. The important thing is that what Polly is saying is that our practical joke, which was a culmination of a campaign of practical jokes against Ms. Cheevy, finally unhinged her. Pushed her over the edge. Caused a major and profound personality change."

"Warped her out," Algie interpreted for Jaws. Algie nodded. "Speaking from personal experience, I'd say it could happen."

"See? It *is* Bentley's fault that I flunked that test," whined Polly.

Everyone ignored her.

"Wow," said Maria softly. "Ms. Cheevy has lost it. She's really and truly lost it."

They all turned at once to look across the room at the teachers' table, strategically located near the front of the lunchroom. Ms. Cheevy was sitting there, staring down at her plate. Considering the noise level of the lunchroom, which had rasped on stronger nerves than hers, she was enduring quite well. Although the occasional crash of a tray to the floor or a fork against a wall made her jump, she wasn't twitching nonstop. In fact, the expression on her face was one of deep thought, of concentration, rather than of random terror.

"Maybe it's temporary," suggested Stacey. "Maybe by tomorrow she'll be her old self again."

They kept on staring.

As if she could feel their eyes upon her, Ms. Cheevy slowly raised her gaze from the contemplation of her lunchroom tray. She turned her head to look back at them. She pushed her glasses higher on the bridge of her nose and peered out from behind them in their direction.

For a long moment she stared across the lunchroom.

She didn't blush. She didn't tremble. She didn't smile nervously, helplessly, or hopelessly.

She stared. Then, still staring, she picked up her knife. Without looking at her plate, she stabbed it viciously downward and came up with a chunk of the caf's mystery meat impaled on the end of it. She held it up. Then she bared big white teeth and bit down and ripped off a hunk like a shark.

CHAPTER

6

It was a sickening sight. Enough to make the weak faint and the strong shudder.

Ms. Cheevy nodded. She'd made her point and was clearly pleased. She turned back to her lunch as if the table of stunned students was no longer important. Less than nothing.

"She's changed. And she's not gonna change back," Algie said wisely.

"We really are in trouble. Big trouble," said Park.

Jordie said, "Perhaps an apology—"

"No way," said Bent.

Now the eyes of everyone around him turned back in his direction. "You wouldn't apologize to Ms. Cheevy?" asked Maria. "Not even to save the rest of us?"

"I think it should be considered," said Jordie.

"An apology *might* work," said Algie.

"No. *No!*" Bent heard his voice go up. "No way! I'd rather die first."

Silence fell over the two tables.

"Another one of your jokes, Bentley?" asked Polly with nasty sweetness.

Jordie said, "Considering the state things have reached, Bentley, I wouldn't make rash statements such as that. However, just to show you that I realize my culpability in this unhappy situation, I am willing to join you in extending our regrets to Ms. Cheevy in an effort to restore her to her normal state."

Park slapped Bentley heartily on the shoulder. "There you go, Bent One. She's gonna go with you, help you out."

Bent looked around at the students surrounding him. Friends.

Former friends, he thought.

He realized he had no choice. Slowly he nodded.

"Okay," he said. "I'll apologize. But I have to tell you now, I think we're making a big mistake."

"Excellent. I suggest we act immediately." Jordie stood up.

Bentley fell back in his chair in disbelief. He clutched his throat. He pretended to gag. "You mean *now*? That's sick. That's sickening. I'm trying to eat lunch here."

"Do it and get it over with," advised Maria. "It'll be easier that way. Then you won't have to think about it."

Nodding, Jordie said, "Exactly. Besides, the longer Ms. Cheevy is in this excessively vengeful state, the more she is reinforced in her student-negative behavior."

Before Jaws could ask, Algie said, "You mean, the more she does this, the more she's gonna like doing it."

"Precisely."

Polly opened her mouth. Bentley held up his hand quickly. "I'm going, I'm going," he said.

He and Jordie walked across the lunchroom. He could feel the two tables behind watching. He forced himself to walk alongside Jordie rather than lagging behind. He didn't want to look like a coward.

"Has anyone ever told you that you should consider the consequences of some of your actions before acting?" asked Jordie.

"I've been told I'm gonna get it if I keep it up, yeah."

Ms. Cheevy's head was down. She didn't seem aware of their approach. Fortunately no one nearby seemed to notice that he, Bentley Jeste, was voluntarily approaching the teachers' table.

"Perhaps this whole incident will have a modifying effect on your behavior, particularly your tendency to formulate crude practical jokes."

"I don't think so," said Bentley. He tried to imagine life without practical jokes. Stupid gags. Clever and devious psych-outs.

No.

But maybe he'd lay off Cheevy. Now and forever.

"Although I will admit," added Jordie in a lower voice as they reached Ms. Cheevy's table, "that I found my participation in the joke enjoyable. Extremely enjoyable."

Bentley couldn't believe he'd heard right. Jordie, class brain and serious student, was saying she'd enjoyed playing a practical joke.

But it was too late to check her words against his hearing. Apology time had come.

They stopped. Jordie cleared her throat. "Um, Ms. Cheevy?"

Ms. Cheevy looked up with a start. Bentley realized once again how tall she was. Maybe the tallest teacher in the school. Maybe the tallest *person* in the school, taller even than the incredible hulking Basement Bart.

"We were wondering if we could have a word with you," Jordie said.

Raising one bushy eyebrow, and swallowing in a way that reminded Bent reassuringly of the old, terrified Ms. Cheevy, the math teacher said, "Certainly."

"Well, what we wanted to say was . . ." Jordie paused, seemingly at a loss for words.

"We're sorry," said Bent. "Like, you know, the jokes. I mean, they were just jokes. They were for fun, you know?"

"Fun," said Ms. Cheevy in her hoarse voice.

"Yeah," said Bent. "You know."

"I'm afraid I don't," said Ms. Cheevy.

"It was an unfortunate attempt to display a sense of humor," said Jordie. "We're sorry that you were not amused. But in fact, we wouldn't have played that joke on you if we didn't like you."

"Yeah!" said Bentley.

"And all those other so-called jokes? Those were out of your deep sense of like for me?" asked Ms. Cheevy.

"Ah, well, yeah," said Bentley.

44

"How nice to know you rate me as among your favorite teachers, Bentley. If, of course, that is measured by the number of what you call jokes you played on me."

"Ah, yeah," said Bent again. This was not going well. Ms. Cheevy, despite a few nervous twitches and one outright flinch when someone dropped yet another tray, was not reverting to her old self. She wasn't talking timid; she was talking tough.

Bent exchanged an agonized glance with Jordie.

She said, "So we hope you'll accept our sincere and profound apologies, Ms. Cheevy. We want you to know it will never happen again."

"How nice," growled Ms. Cheevy.

Growled? Bent shook his head. Was he hearing right?

"I of course accept your apology. I'm a teacher. I have to set a good example. It wouldn't be setting a good example not to accept your apology." Ms. Cheevy turned back to her lunch. She picked up her fork. She stabbed the peas several times with frightening vigor. Then she said, in her new, nasty growl, "But forgiveness or no, I wouldn't forget to do my homework if I were you. All twenty-six pages of it."

Jordie and Bentley stood for a moment in stunned disbelief.

Then Jordie said, "Thank you, Ms. Cheevy. I believe we understand what you've just told us to do with our apology."

Ms. Cheevy stabbed some more peas. "I believe you do," she said.

45

A tray fell, a chair thumped over, and a girl shrieked. Reflexively Ms. Cheevy jerked around in her chair.

Reflexively Bent acted. A moment later Jordie was dragging him away from the table.

"I can't believe you did that," she said through her teeth.

"*Aaaaaah!*" Bent heard Ms. Cheevy scream behind him. He heard the sound of her chair being knocked over as she leaped to her feet.

She'd found the rubber cockroach he'd dropped into her coleslaw. Bent smiled with satisfaction. "Believe it," he said to Jordie. "You heard what she said. We apologized for nothing. She's out to get us, no matter what."

He stopped and faced Jordie, catching her by the arm. "This," he said, "means war."

CHAPTER
7

Bentley was startled by the knock on his bedroom door. He was deep in one of his gag catalogs. War required strategy. Planning.

Money.

He could manage the first two, but what about the third?

The knock sounded again.

"Come in already," he snapped. "Quit banging on the door."

His father looked into the room. "Is that any way to greet guests?"

"Yes," Bent said crossly.

"It's okay, Mr. Jeste," he heard Jordie say behind his father. "We've got a test, and I bet Bent's already studying for it."

"That'll be the day," said Bent's father, but he went away without further comment.

"What're *you* doing here?" said Bent.

"You said it meant war. After the events of the last day and a half, I'm willing to concede that you're right."

"Big thrills," said Bent.

He had declared it a war, but he clearly hadn't been the only one. Since Bent and Jordie had walked away from Cheevy's table in the lunchroom to report the failure of their mission to the other students, Ms. Cheevy had given out thirty-six math problems for homework, assigned seven chapters of reading, and told the students they were going to have to do reports on famous mathematicians. She'd also given another pop quiz, which everybody had failed.

"We just don't seem to be concentrating, do we, students?" she said cheerfully, handing out the tests. "More homework should do the trick!"

Bent had been too beaten down to even groan.

And his class wasn't the only one. The Mad Math Teacher was doing it to all her classes. No one was escaping.

And thanks in large part to Polly's big mouth, everyone was blaming Bent.

Remembering this, Bent said, "You're not going to start talking about actions and consequences again, are you?"

"No."

With a scowl Bent went back to the catalog.

Jordie sat down in the chair in the corner of Bent's room and looked thoughtfully around. She wasn't quite sure what she had expected. A moat with piranhas in it?

The world's largest collection of fake joke insects? A room decorated in Early Weird?

The only strange thing that she could see was a hand emerging from a sleeve emerging from the closed top drawer of Bent's dresser. The collection of rubber insects on the top of his bookcase looked pretty normal. The gag puddle of vomit in the corner of his room with the candy wrapper stuck in it was gross, but it was an old-fashioned trick.

In fact, apart from the black curtains on Bent's windows, the only other odd thing about his room was the huge collection of books on gags, jokes, strange-but-true incidents, and magic tricks that lined his shelves.

"Are you interested in pursuing a career as a magician?" she asked him.

He said, "Maybe." He didn't look up.

"Can you do magic tricks?" she asked.

"A few," said Bent. He put the catalog down. "I just got the books so that I could use magic tricks to psych people out, see?"

"I see," said Jordie. Then she said, "What I'd like to discuss today is joining forces. If this is war with Ms. Cheevy, you can't fight it alone."

"Tell me about it," he muttered.

"So, count me in," she said simply.

"What?"

"I would like to help you wage a campaign against Cheevy," said Jordie, sounding almost but not quite normal. She paused and scowled to herself. "I flunked that second pop quiz, too. Not to mention that she's a crummy teacher."

Bent brushed the crummy-teacher objection aside and focused on the important fact at hand. "You want to go in with me? Help smoke out Cheevy?" He suddenly felt more hopeful. Much as he hated to admit it, he admired Jordie's brains. And she'd been a useful partner in the prank that had started the whole mess.

"Yes. I want to pursue, I believe, your life of crime."

"Hey! I'm no criminal," said Bent, his warm-and-fuzzy, friendly thoughts forgotten.

"I didn't mean it the way it sounded. It's just that I'm so used to being above reproach. I find your approach to life compelling. Exhilarating. I like it."

Bent wasn't quite sure what she'd said, but he decided that in the interest of pursuing justice against Cheevy, it was good.

"Deal," he said. "You're in." He grabbed a couple of catalogs and pitched them to her. "Start going through these. And start thinking of some way to make the students at Graveyard School Cheevy-proof . . . now and forever."

Ms. Cheevy slammed open the classroom door.

She peered inside. Although she was the new, meaner version of Chicken Cheevy, she clearly meant to take no chances.

Or prisoners, either.

"Pop quiz," she announced with cheerful, spiteful

glee, as soon as she had ascertained that Bent was in his seat and not lurking behind the door.

No one moved. The class was unnaturally quiet, except for a horrified gasp from Polly Hannah.

Ms. Cheevy swept into the room. She was in her usual unfashionable attire: a long skirt, a baggy jacket, and a high-necked blouse. Her hair was straggling and hung in Medusa-like strands around her face. Her stockings were thick and brightly colored—a solid shade today. Her big feet were in big black shoes that looked sort of the way Bent imagined witches' shoes looked.

Any feelings of remorse he might have had about what he and Jordie were planning vanished.

"The test will be on the nine chapters I gave you to review last night," said Ms. Cheevy.

Polly waved her hand wildly, desperately.

"Yes, Polly?" said Ms. Cheevy with gentle menace.

"I didn't get to read all the chapters," Polly said. "My mother made me turn out the light and go to sleep."

"Ah. Sleep. You know, as a teacher, I've had many a sleepless night worrying about class the next day. Particularly since I started teaching here. Perhaps you can appreciate that, Polly."

"Yes, but—"

"Good." Ms. Cheevy's voice hardened. "It's not my problem that you didn't do your homework, Polly. Good students do their homework. Now: Question one."

Polly whimpered. But she obeyed.

Bentley smiled to himself. Polly was the only one who

wasn't included in today's joke. Too bad she hadn't been nicer to him in the past.

He took out his pencil and carefully extracted a piece of paper from his notebook.

Had Ms. Cheevy been paying attention, she might have noticed that everybody in the whole class had taken out the exact same kind of paper—everybody but Polly.

But Ms. Cheevy was standing at the window, looking out. Frowning.

Her sudden movement caught Bent's attention. She leaped back and hastily closed the blinds. Quickly she turned and kept reciting the questions of the pop quiz aloud—ten in all.

Ten impossible questions. No kid could have known the answers. Not even Jordie.

Had Ms. Cheevy not been distracted by whatever she had seen outside the window, she might have noticed that no one in her class seemed particularly concerned by the quiz.

They wrote their answers quickly. Quietly. Cheerfully.

When they were finished, they handed the tests to their teacher without a single murmur of protest.

Ms. Cheevy went to her desk and opened the big, battered old briefcase she always carried. She stuffed the test papers inside.

"I'll have your grades for you tomorrow," she promised.

She reached for the top drawer of her desk, and said, "And now for a little classwork, just as soon as I assign homework. I think the next nine chapters would be appropriate." She stopped. "Of course, Polly, that means you have a few more than that to do, if you want to catch up."

"Yes, Ms. Cheevy," said Polly, her spirit broken.

Ms. Cheevy smiled. Then she stopped.

Perhaps some inkling of the class's silent declaration of war had penetrated her senses. She frowned.

Bent held his breath.

Ms. Cheevy narrowed her eyes. "And now," she said, "for some classwork—"

She opened the drawer as she spoke.

And began to scream.

CHAPTER

8

"Aaaaaagagggagag!"

The spider that had leaped out of her drawer clung to her face.

She slapped at it wildly. She fell back against the blackboard.

The spider slipped off her face and clung to her dress.

She did a crazy dance, shaking her skirt and screaming. When it fell to the floor, she began to stomp on it.

No one in the class moved.

No one said a word.

Except Polly.

Polly began to laugh. She laughed and laughed.

She was still laughing when Ms. Cheevy stopped stomping on the rubber spider and bent to pick it up from the floor.

Bent blinked. He blinked again. Was it his imagination or had Ms. Cheevy's hair moved? Had she just that moment acquired a *receding* hairline?

"I can't believe she fell for the old rubber spider trick," Park said to Bent out of the side of his mouth.

"New spider," returned Bent.

Holding the spider by one of its slimy rubber legs, Mrs. Cheevy advanced on Polly. "You find this funny?" she snarled.

Polly stopped laughing in mid-ha.

She gulped. "N-No," she said.

"You're laughing," said Ms. Cheevy.

"N-No," said Polly even more uncertainly.

"This isn't *your* spider, is it, Polly?"

"No!" Polly sounded much more sure of herself this time.

"Ah," said Ms. Cheevy. She held the spider up. "Anybody know where this spider came from?"

"Up your nose," muttered Jordie clearly.

Ms. Cheevy swiveled in Jordie's direction. For a long moment the two locked eyes. Then Ms. Cheevy said, "Since no one claims it . . ." She marched back to her desk and took out the scissors. She held up the rubber spider in one hand and the scissors in the other.

Bent gulped. *Not my poor, defenseless, expensive new rubber spider! She wouldn't, would she?*

She would. She did.

With a mean smile on her face, Ms. Cheevy began to cut the spider to bits. First she cut off its legs, one at a time, a little bit of each leg at a time. Next she cut its body into small, jagged chunks. She let the pieces fall in a rubbery shower into her garbage can. She stared down into the rubber spider's grave for a long moment with a peculiar expression. Almost absently she reached up and scratched her head.

Her hair moved. Bent was sure he saw it move. But before he could say anything, Ms. Cheevy wheeled around and drove all thoughts from his mind.

She smiled.

"Pop quiz," she said. "Question one: How many pieces did I just *divide* the spider into?"

"It's not working," said Bent.

"Not yet," answered Jordie. She didn't seem to notice the glares and mutters of the students they were passing in the hall.

Bent kept his head down. That way he couldn't see. And he tried to pretend he couldn't hear. But he had a feeling his life was in danger.

"I feel in danger," he said.

"Well, you aren't endangered," said Jordie.

"Listen, I'm the only one of me there is. Therefore, if anything happens to me, I become extinct. That makes me endangered," said Bent.

"You're losing it, Bent. You aren't in danger. You aren't endangered. You're just paranoid."

"No. People are staring at me. At us. And they are talking about me. And you. Trust me on this."

They'd reached the front door. Safely.

"Don't look back," Satchel Paige, the famous pitcher, had said. "You never know what might be gaining on you."

Bent didn't look back. He took the stairs two at a time and didn't stop moving until he reached the bottom. Then he stopped.

The bus was waiting in front of the school.

It was full of kids. Lots of kids. Lots of unfriendly kids. Some of them were looking in his direction. As he stood there, more and more faces turned his way.

"Hey," said Bent suddenly. "You walk home, don'tcha? I'll walk with you."

Jordie shrugged. "Okay."

"So this is not working," Bent said again as soon as they'd made it a safe distance from the school and the bus.

"Things like this take time. Rome wasn't built in a day."

"We're not building Rome here, Jordie. We're trying to save our own hides. Get out of math alive. Not to mention the school." Bent checked over his shoulder to make sure no irate students—or crazed math teachers—were trailing him. "So far, I've put a cockroach in her lunch . . ." He paused thoughtfully. "Although you might not notice it was a *fake* cockroach in the food here. Anyway, the cockroach, the spider-in-the-drawer trick, the Vaseline-on-the-classroom-doorknob trick, and the test-with-the-disappearing-ink trick."

"I get your point," said Jordie. "But it's only been a couple of days. Besides, she just got our test. That should do something."

"I hope so," said Bent, " 'cause no one is laughing at my jokes anymore. I'm not having any fun. Ms. Cheevy is ruining my life!"

She closed the curtains. She turned on her desk lamp and put the stack of papers next to it. But she didn't look at the papers right away. Propping her elbow on the desk and her chin on her hand, she sat staring at the curtains.

Ms. Cheevy lived, like a teacher in a bad old movie, in a small apartment with only two windows on the third floor of a four-story apartment building. Although Grove Hill was the home of the strangest elementary school in the known universe, it was not what most people would call a high-crime area. The last crime wave had been when someone went on a rampage and jammed gum in all the parking meters around the courthouse. The sheriff had investigated the usual suspects but made no arrests, although he did issue a sternly worded statement about the need for gum control.

But the math teacher didn't seem comforted by the low crime rate of the town. Although she lived on the third floor and although only one of her two windows could be reached from the fire escape, she had bars on both windows. She also had a burglar alarm system that would go off if anyone tried to raise the windows or open the door.

The curtains on the windows were thick. There were big locks on every door in the apartment, too.

The burglar bars, the burglar alarm, and the heavy brown curtains were her big decorating items. When she'd come to Grove Hill the year before, she'd rented the apartment with the furniture in it, not even arguing with the landlord about the rent. The furniture was old and dark brown: dark brown wood, dark brown fabric. The carpet was a mixture of brown and beige that didn't show dirt because it looked like dirt. The lamps were dim.

The place was neat, as neat as a hotel room after the cleaning staff had been through. It didn't look as if anyone lived there: no pictures on the tables, no pictures on the walls, nothing personal. If she walked out and closed the door and never came back, the next person to walk in would be able to tell nothing about her, except that she was paranoid.

The grim little apartment didn't seem to bother Ms. Cheevy, though. She didn't even seem to notice it as she sat staring at the closed curtain. Her gimlet eyes were almost dreamy.

A sound at the fire-escape window drove the dreamy look from her face. With uncanny quickness for so large and clumsy a woman, she leaped across the room and pressed herself against the wall next to the curtain.

Then a cat began to howl outside, shouting insults at another cat below, which howled back.

Still cautious, Ms. Cheevy moved the curtain aside a fraction. Satisfied that it really was a cat, she let the curtain drop back into place and walked heavily back to her desk.

Looking down, she seemed to notice for the first time the big shoes on her big feet. She sat down and kicked them off with an impatient, disgusted sound.

"Someday," she said aloud, "I'm going to have decent shoes again." And she wondered for the thousandth time why it was so hard to find decent women's shoes in anything but petite.

Bah. She hated the whole idea of petite. Women came in all shapes and sizes, including large. But what did the makers of shoes and dresses do? Make small clothes and try to convince women that it was they who were too big, not the clothes that were too small and all wrong.

With a scowl, Ms. Cheevy turned back to the papers on her desk. She opened the drawer, hesitating only a millisecond as she remembered the spider that had jumped out of her school desk drawer during second-period math that morning.

She rummaged for her red grading pencil, a small smile on her face. The spider. She knew who was behind that. In fact, she knew much, much more than the students realized. Although she appeared to be clueless, she was actually very observant.

And now that she had decided to drop her timid act, she was almost beginning to enjoy being a teacher—especially now that the students had decided to fight back. Nothing like a good war. . . .

She found the pencil. She closed the drawer and opened the second-period math folder with the tests in it.

The top piece of paper was blank. Someone must have handed in two sheets of paper. Impatiently she pushed it to one side.

She frowned. The second sheet was blank, too. And the third. And the fourth.

Flipping through the entire folder, she discovered that every single sheet of paper was blank except Polly Hannah's.

How had they done that? The tests had all had writing on them when her students had handed them in. She was sure of that. She was equally sure that no one from the class could have come anywhere near her book bag, which she kept closely guarded.

Cunning little beasts, she thought. Smarter than she'd given them credit for. And, of course, it would be worse now that Bent and Jordie seemed to have joined forces. Each of them was smart, each of them was twisted in his or her own way, the way most truly smart and creative people were.

It would never do to underestimate the opposition. That was the number one rule for survival.

Suddenly she laughed. Polly Hannah was the class prig. And clearly she, Ms. Cheevy, wasn't the only one who thought so.

She studied Polly's paper for a long, long time. Then she looked at the blank tests once again.

She laughed again, a laugh of diabolical pleasure. Then she wrote a big red A at the top of Polly's test. She wrote a big red F at the top of each of the others.

Tomorrow she would announce that she was counting the grades double for this particular pop quiz.

Polly would be pleased and no doubt make herself odious to the rest of her classmates. And they?

They couldn't complain, could they? Because then they'd have to confess that they'd turned in, somehow, blank tests.

"Never underestimate the power of a teacher," murmured Ms. Cheevy.

She could hardly wait to see their faces the next morning.

CHAPTER
9

"She flamed us," said Jordie. She shook her head in rueful admiration. "Totally."

"She killed us," said Maria, pushing her dark bangs back in agitation.

Polly said, "*I* got an A."

"Go choke on a cracker," snapped Stacey. She looked less pulled-together than usual.

Even Jaws seemed a little off his feed, rejecting the third chunk of corn bread that Algie had shoved his way. Only Jordie seemed unaffected by the aftermath of math class that morning.

"We've got to do something fast," said Jordie. "Let her know that we're not intimidated."

She frowned. She looked down at the end of the table, where Bent was hunched over his lunch tray. "Eat it, throw up in it, or give it away, Bent. We need your help."

Bent straightened up. "I'm thinking, I'm thinking," he

complained. "Don't keep interrupting me. You're ruining my concentration."

Polly said, "I don't think you should do anything to Ms. Cheevy. After all, if you hadn't been so awful to her—"

Standing up, Maria leaned forward and slapped her palms down on the table. "Keep talking and you'll start walking," she threatened Polly.

"I'm entitled to my opinion," said Polly.

Suddenly Bent leaped up. He grabbed Polly's tray and began to charge across the lunchroom with it.

"Hey!" said Polly. "Hey! Give me that." She jumped up and ran after him.

Bent let Polly catch up with him just as he reached the teachers' table, where Ms. Cheevy was sitting with Mr. Lucre. Mr. Lucre was talking.

He stopped to take a breath and Bent put Polly's tray down on the table across from Ms. Cheevy.

Ms. Cheevy watched him calmly.

"Polly wants to sit with you," announced Bent. "To thank you for being such a good teacher and making it possible for her to do so well in math."

"Well, well, well," said Mr. Lucre, butting in. "How delightful. How unusual. How, er, nice."

"Yes," said Bent. "We all thought so."

He gave Polly, who'd turned a sickly green beneath her pink cheeks, a thump of the back. "Enjoy, Polly," he said.

"Sit down, Polly," said Ms. Cheevy.

Polly looked wildly around. Bent gave her a big smile.

"Speak, Polly," he said, and walked away as Mr. Lucre pulled a chair up so that Polly could sit at the end of the table between him and the math teacher.

"Excellent work, Bent," said Jordie when Bent returned.

"Yes," said Bent. "I know."

His moment of brilliance had restored his confidence. Renewed his inner resources. Made him believe in himself again.

He sat down. He leaned forward. "This is the plan," he said. "And it's good. Very good. So good you're gonna die laughing.

" 'Cause it's a killer."

After school, Bent, Jordie, Maria, Algie, Park, and Stacey all met on the front steps to work on their plan. They sat and talked casually while keeping an eye out for teachers—one teacher in particular.

"We've got work to do here," Bent said. "Now, remember, we are sweet students. Star scholars. Perfect pupils. The teacher is always right."

"I'm gonna be sick," Jordie muttered.

Maria shook her head. She stuck out her lower lip and blew her bangs up off her face. "I'll do it. But I don't understand it."

"It's as easy as two plus two," said Bent. He saw Jordie open her mouth to say something more mathematically correct and hurried on. "We want to lull her into thinking that we've given up. Make her let down her guard. Let her think she's achieved her goal and broken our spirits."

"That part won't be hard," said Stacey. "And when my parents see my math grade, it's not the only thing that's gonna get broken."

"Good, good. That's the idea," Bent said encouragingly.

Just then Polly walked out of school. She spotted the gang and walked up to them. "What are you guys up to now?" she asked pointedly.

Bent studied her for a long moment.

Jordie said, "I don't think you should tell her, Bent. After all, she *is* the teacher's pet."

"You don't think I'd tell on you, do you?" asked Polly.

"I think you'd sell your own dog for a good grade," said Stacey.

"We don't have a dog anymore," said Polly. "She—"

Bent held up his hand. "Can we trust you, Polly? You won't go straight to Ms. Cheevy and tell her?"

"I promise. Cross my heart," said Polly quickly.

"What heart?" muttered Maria.

But after a quick glance at Jordie, Bent nodded. "You're in," he said. "What're we're gonna do is lull Ms. Cheevy into a false sense of security. Then *bam*, we let her have it!" Bent drove his fist into the palm of his hand to demonstrate.

Polly waited a moment. Then she said, "Is that all? That's the plan?"

"You don't like it?" asked Bent.

"But you didn't tell me what it was. What's the joke? What are you going to *do*?" demanded Polly.

"Oh. That." Bent looked left. He looked right. He checked back over his shoulder. Then he motioned everybody to come closer. "Next Friday afternoon, exactly one week from today, one of us will stay after school to get some help with our math homework. We will keep Ms. Cheevy late. So late that everyone will have left the school. Everyone always takes off early on Fridays anyway. Even Basement Bart. Then, after she finishes helping whoever it is, that person will ask Cheevy to walk them to the front door and let them out, in case the school is locked up. Since it probably will be, she'll agree. She'll see her student leave. She'll walk back to her classroom. And that's when she'll meet . . . the ghost!"

"Yeah, right," said Polly.

"Seriously," said Bent. "I've got it all figured out."

"Where are you going to get the ghost?" Polly shifted her books to one arm and put her hand on her hip.

"One of us is going to be the ghost." Bent paused. His eyes suddenly gleamed. "And I know just the person."

"Who?" asked Polly.

"You," said Bent.

"Me? Not me!" Polly's voice went up in horror.

"Yes," said Bent. "You."

Jordie said, in her usual measured way, "What you propose, Bent, makes a certain amount of sense. If Polly

69

refuses to be the ghost, we can assume that she was not telling us the truth and that she is going to rat us out to Ms. Cheevy or Dr. Morthouse."

"Wait a minute," protested Polly, her voice getting even shriller.

"On the other hand, if she wants to prove that she is in fact in league with us," Jordie went on, "she will help us and be a part of our attempts to scare Ms. Cheevy back to the shadow that was her former self."

"Makes sense," said Park. "Sort of."

Maria said, "Like a test. You think you can pass this test, Polly? Or would you rather live and *die* a teacher's pet?"

Polly looked around at Bent, Jordie, Maria, Stacey, Park, and Algie. "What about Jaws?" she said. "He's not here. I vote for Jaws to do it."

"Trying to rat out Jaws now?" Stacey asked sweetly.

"No! Of course not!" Polly licked her lips. "Will I be wearing a, like, costume? A disguise?"

Bent nodded. "Of course. Your own mother won't recognize you, even if she was a ghost, too."

"And I just jump out and scare Ms. Cheevy. That's it?"

After thinking it over a moment, Bent said, "As far as I can see, that's it. It's pretty easy. The hard part is the prep work, which we'll all have to do."

But Polly wasn't interested in the preparations. She was focusing on not being called a traitor and not getting caught. "So I put on the costume, I jump out, and I leave. That's all?"

Looking at Polly, Bent suffered a momentary qualm. Could she do it? Or would she chicken out at the last minute and blow the whole thing?

"That's all. But I don't know. Maybe we should—" he began.

Polly cut him off. "Okay. I'll do it. But if I get caught, you're going to be sorry. All of you."

Bent said, "I'm a pro, Polly, remember? Pros don't get caught."

Polly snorted. Even her snorts had a faintly nasal, whiny sound. "Tell that to Dr. Morthouse." She turned and walked away.

Jordie said, "Maybe we shouldn't let Polly do this after all. She could try to double-cross us and ruin everything. I don't trust her."

"Who does?" said Bent. "Who trusts anybody?"

CHAPTER

10

"Seven days make one weak," Bent moaned to Jordie as they staggered toward Graveyard School the following Friday. "That's *w-e-a-k,* in case you're wondering."

Jordie didn't bother to acknowledge the lame attempt at humor. She just shifted her overstuffed backpack and transferred the bulging bag she was carrying from one hand to the other. "What have you got in here, Bent? The kitchen sink?"

"Props," said Bent. "We want this to be totally realistic, don't we?"

"True," said Jordie. They trudged onward. While Jordie agreed with Bent's theory that the fewer people actually involved with carrying out the plan Let's Scare Ms. Cheevy to Death the better, she regretted that it meant that only he and she were responsible for everything.

Reflecting on Bent's feeble joke, Jordie was forced to acknowledge that it had been a long week. While she was used to being a model student, she wasn't used to having to *try* to be a model student. Thinking about acting normal made her feel really weird.

But if it was hard for her, it must have been even harder for the rest of the class to sit quietly, do all the homework, take three pop quizes without complaining, and get test papers back with big red low grades at the top without even the whisper of a protest.

It would have been a sad, sad sight if Jordie hadn't known that it was for a good cause.

Naturally Ms. Cheevy had been suspicious. Her eyes had been on continual scan mode, searching everywhere for the least sign of trouble. By the third day of Good Behavior Week, she'd taken to opening drawers and looking inside in a way that was almost disappointed.

She'd seemed puzzled. More than once Jordie had looked up to see Cheevy studying her and other members of the class with a curious expression.

But in the last couple of days, she'd actually seemed to accept the fact that she had won. That they were beaten. The night before, she'd even given a homework assignment that bore some resemblance to normality.

Did Ms. Cheevy think they were so easy? Jordie was surprised. Somehow she'd hoped that Chicken Cheevy had had hidden depths—deeper reserves of suspicion and paranoia.

Too bad.

But at last the week was over. Today was the day. Revenge was going to be sweet.

"I suspect that Polly will call in sick today," Jordie said.

"Not if she doesn't want to call in dead on Monday," said Bent, "which is what I told her when I called this morning." He paused. "Of course, first I pretended that I thought Mrs. Hannah was Polly and said, 'Hi, Polly! Are you going to fake being sick today like we planned so we can skip school?' "

Jordie stopped. "You know," she said, "I continually underestimate you. That was brilliant. Truly sneaky and low."

"Thank you," said Bent.

Graveyard School had come into sight. It was an imposing building, especially because it was framed by the graves that marched up the hill behind it. For a moment Bent thought he heard the low moaning of the wind that always seemed to be blowing through the old tombstones. It sent a cold finger of apprehension down his neck.

The sound of the wind seemed to turn into an evil chuckle.

"Did you hear that?" Bent asked.

"What?" asked Jordie.

I hope I'm not developing a conscience or something, thought Bent. Aloud he said, "Never mind."

The first-graders, huddled at the bottom of the steps where they always waited, backed away at the approach of the two sixth-graders. Bent and Jordie barely noticed them.

The door swung open when they reached the top of the stairs.

"Well, well, well," said an all-too-familiar voice. "What have we here?"

"Dr. Morthouse," said Bent, coming to a sudden stop. How could he have forgotten about the principal's uncanny ability to turn up where she was least wanted? Dr. Morthouse: on the Ten Least Wanted list.

Fortunately Jordie seemed unmoved by Dr. Morthouse's presence. "Why do you always stand just inside the front door and watch us?" she asked.

Dr. Morthouse gave Jordie a sharp look, but Jordie's tone was detached and her expression merely interested.

"I have my reasons," said Dr. Morthouse.

She and Jordie eyed each other for a long moment. Then Dr. Morthouse said, "Lots of homework?"

"What?" said Bent.

"You're carrying quite a lot there."

"Oh . . . uh . . . yes. . . . Homework. . . . Gotta do that homework . . . ," Bent babbled.

In a bored voice Jordie said, "It's a stupid special project."

"I'm sure it will only be as stupid as you make it," purred Dr. Morthouse. She smiled. Something silver glinted in her mouth. And then she stepped aside and let them pass.

When they were out of earshot, Bent said, "Whew."

"Shhh," said Jordie. "She has hearing like a bat."

Bent wasn't about to argue. They went the rest of the way in silence.

* * *

"I still don't think you should be in here," said Polly.

"Chill, okay?" said Bent, hoping he wasn't turning red. His visions of pulling a practical joke involving the girls' bathroom were fading fast in the cold, blue-tiled light of reality.

"Are you *sure* this is how this disgusting goop goes on?" asked Polly.

"I'm sure, I'm sure, okay?" Bent didn't want to tell Polly that he'd special-ordered all of the stuff and had never used it before in his life. And that the ghost outfit had wiped out his life savings.

"I don't see why Jordie can't be the one who does this."

"Because," said Bent, trying to keep his voice calm, "she's the decoy. If I went to Ms. Cheevy and I said I wanted to discuss mathematics with her, she'd know something was up."

"I guess," said Polly.

Bent continued to apply the Guaranteed Ghost makeup while Polly watched him in the mirror above the middle sink.

Somehow coming into the girls' bathroom because he had to had taken the fun out of it, even though his being there was bothering Polly. But he hadn't been able to talk her into going into the boys' bathroom.

"Stand still," Bent said.

Polly said crossly, "You said I was going to be a ghost. This isn't a ghost outfit!"

"Yes it is."

"I want a sheet," said Polly. "I want something that will cover my face."

"Ghosts don't wear sheets. People pretending to be ghosts wear sheets. Ghosts can wear whatever they want, but they prefer wearing what they were wearing when they died. Now, will you please stand still?" Bent smeared more goo on Polly's face.

"Yuck!" wailed Polly.

"Shhh!" whispered Bent. "You want Basement Bart to hear you?"

"You said everyone went home early on Fridays. Even Basement Bart."

"Of course," Bent said hastily. "But better safe than sorry." Bent wasn't at all sure that Basement Bart ever went home. But that didn't bear thinking about now.

"There." Bent stepped back and Polly leaned forward to inspect her ghost makeup.

Bent took the opportunity to sneak a quick look at the row of stalls. Everything looked pretty ordinary. And just as messy as the boys' bathroom at the end of the day. There was even graffiti scratched into the paint. Was that his name he saw? He edged closer.

"Now what?" said Polly, giving him a suspicious look.

"Right. Sorry." Bent tore himself away from his examination of the mysterious girls' bathroom and bent down to rummage through the bags and backpacks on the floor around Polly.

A little while later, Polly disappeared.

In her place a pale, pale child with faintly glowing skin

looked back at herself in the mirror. Her eyes were rimmed with red. So were her ghastly pale lips. Her hair seemed to float around her shoulders. Her long, flowing, old-fashioned clothes, borrowed from Jordie's mother's hippie college days, floated weirdly around her body.

"How do you make my clothes do that?" asked Polly.

"Some kind of spray," said Bent. "It's sort of like the reverse of static cling, or something."

"I hope it's not toxic," said Polly. But she didn't sound as grouchy. She was staring at herself in fascination.

"Umm," said Bent. Then he held up a small light. "When we turn this on you in the dark, you will look really gruesome. I'll set it up. It's battery operated, so when you want to disappear, just step on the switch and the light will go off, plunging you into darkness. You won't be visible without the light."

He took a small fan out of one of the bags. "We'll set this up on the floor near you. That will make you look even more floating and spooky. And even though it is starting to get dark outside, we should pull down all the blinds. Of course, knowing Cheevy, she'll probably have most of them pulled down already. Also, we should turn out the hall lights, and the ones in the classroom. I'll tape the light switch in the classroom so it won't turn on."

He looked at his watch. "C'mon. It's time." Hurrying toward the door, he leaned out. The halls were still, dark, and empty. He motioned to Polly and they stepped out into the hall.

"Whatever you do," he said in a low voice, "don't

move and don't say a word. Just sort of stand there. That's even scarier. She might try to talk to you or something, but don't answer. Oh yeah, and don't let her get between you and the door."

Polly's eyes widened. "But—"

"Shhh!"

Down at the other end of the hall, Ms. Cheevy came out of her room.

Bent jerked Polly back inside the bathroom. "That was close," he said. "Jordie's a little ahead of schedule."

They waited another minute. Bent stuck his head out into the hall again. It was empty. "Now!" Bent said.

They took off down the hall for Ms. Cheevy's room. Operation Let's Scare the Teacher to Death was about to begin.

CHAPTER
11

Jordie had done her job. The classroom was empty.

Polly allowed herself to be arranged on a chair on the side of the room away from the windows. Bent turned the fan on and fixed the light switches. He raced back out and into a niche beside the water fountain just as the silhouette of Ms. Cheevy reappeared at the far end of the hall.

Bent looked at his watch. Was he a professional, or what?

He settled back into his corner to wait.

She walked slowly. She stayed close to one wall. She stopped from time to time.

Bent contemplated again what a chicken his math teacher was. *Maybe*, he thought, *she was raised in a haunted house.*

He hoped so.

At last she reached the door.

She pushed it open. She went inside. Bent leaped out

and turned off the lights in the hall so it was in almost total darkness.

There was a long moment of silence.

Bent waited.

"Aaaaaaaahnnnnnnnnnnooooooooaaaaaahh!"

Ms. Cheevy was screaming. She screamed more loudly than Bent had ever heard her scream. She screamed more loudly than Bent had ever heard anyone scream. She screamed more loudly than Bent thought was humanly possible. She screamed and screamed. Bent heard the sound of someone crashing against the door.

Then there was another crash.

And silence.

Silence?

"Uh-oh," said Bent. But before he could say anything more, someone else began to scream. It sounded like a teakettle gone berserk.

"Eeeeeeeeeh!"

The door to Ms. Cheevy's classroom flew open. Polly stood in the doorway, her eyes wide in the red rim of makeup, her mouth a ghastly dark emptiness rimmed with red where Bent had painted her lips and blacked out her teeth.

"Eeeek! Euuuuuwwww! Sheeeee's Dead!"

Bent leaped out from his hiding place and raced forward. He grabbed Polly. She flailed wildly and punched him in the eye.

"Hey!" he said. "Shhh." He dragged her out into the hall.

Polly's unearthly glow faded in the darkness of the hallway. He could barely see her dim, agitated outline.

"Stop screaming!" Bent said in Polly's ear. "Calm down."

"She . . . she . . . she . . . ," gasped Polly.

"It's okay. Stay here." Bent ran forward and peered into the classroom. He could vaguely make out a dark shape on the floor by the desk.

He reached up and fumbled with the light. After several attempts, he ripped the tape off and flipped the light on.

Bent walked slowly forward. A pair of legs, wearing thick striped stockings and funny black shoes, was sticking out from behind the far side of the desk.

"Geez, Polly, what happened?" he said.

He heard Polly stumble to the doorway and stop. "She . . . she . . . she . . ." Polly gulped. "She just fell down." Her voice dropped to a whisper. "She's not . . . dead . . . is she?"

Bent walked a few steps closer. He looked down at the feet. Then he slowly shook his head. "I don't believe this," he said. He turned. He bit his lip and clenched his fists tightly at his sides. He said slowly, "She's dead. Ms. Cheevy is dead. You've killed her."

"I didn't do it!" Polly shrieked. "You made me! It's not my fault!"

"What are we going to do?" asked Bent.

"I didn't do it," Polly said more softly.

Bent looked at Polly. Polly rushed forward and grabbed Bent's arm. "You made me. You've got to help me."

"What can I do?" asked Bent.

"Please?" asked Polly. "We're in this together. We have to stick together. . . . I'd do the same for you."

"You would?"

"I would. I promise I would. Anything. Whatever you say. Just . . ."

Bent smiled.

Polly suddenly stepped back. A puzzled expression crossed her face.

Bent's smile widened into a grin of total triumph. "Gotcha," he said. "Teacher's pet. And you fell for it."

"What're you talking about?" Polly said shakily.

Bent pointed at the legs in the striped stockings and funny black shoes. "You can get up now, Jordie."

"*What?*" shrieked Polly.

Bent said, "It was a setup. Ms. Cheevy has already gone home. She—"

Polly leaped forward and took a wild swing at Bent. He dodged, but not quickly enough. Her fist caught him squarely in the middle. "*Oof,*" he choked out, doubling over. Polly began to pound on his head and shoulders with her fists. "You . . . you . . . you pig! You jerk! You . . ."

"Jordie was in on it, too. Share your feelings with her, okay?" said Bent, trying to protect himself.

"I'll get you for this. You are dead meat. Roadkill. You are going to be so sorry. I'm gonna make you . . ." Polly was gasping and pounding on Bent, who, still doubled over and trying to catch his breath, was trying to get out of her way.

"Hey, it was a joke, okay? Jordie, could—Oww!—I have some help here? *Owww!* Hey, Jordie . . ."

Polly somehow connected with his stomach again. Hard.

"Jordie!" said Bent.

Jordie didn't move.

Polly stopped pounding on Bent for a moment and bent over to catch her own breath. Bent quickly dodged back and around the desk out of range.

"Jordie," he said, dropping down on his knees beside the body. "Joke's over. Get . . ."

His voice trailed off. He leaned forward. He scrambled backward, grabbing the desk for support as he pulled himself to his feet.

Polly chopped him in the side but he didn't notice.

"It's impossible," he said hoarsely. "It can't be."

Something in his voice stopped Polly in midpunch. "What?"

"She's dead," said Bent. "She's really dead."

He was staring down at the body on the floor next to the desk.

"It's Ms. Cheevy," said Bent. The room was spinning. He could hear his own voice, far away and funny. "It's her. She really is dead!"

"No way I'm gonna fall for this again!" shrieked Polly. "You are sick! Sick. *Sick!* And if you think—"

"I knew it," a voice said from the door of the classroom. "I'm too late. I don't believe this. After all that work. It was Basement Bart. I got trapped in the girls' bathroom at the other end of the hall."

Dressed in clothes like Ms. Cheevy would wear, including striped stockings and funny black shoes, Jordie stood in the door of the classroom.

Polly and Bent faced Jordie wordlessly. Bent tried to say something, but no sound came out.

"What?" said Jordie. "Bent, I'm truly, terribly sorry."

Polly said, "Let me see her." She turned and pushed Bent to one side and looked down.

Ms. Cheevy lay there, her hands at her throat, her eyes closed. She didn't move. She didn't breathe.

Polly said, "It is her. It *is* her!"

Jordie looked down for the first time and saw the feet sticking out from behind the desk. The color drained from her face.

"No," she said, and was across the room in one bound.

She looked down. She looked up. She looked all around. Then she looked down again. "It can't be," Jordie said. "It's impossible! What's she doing here?"

"I don't know," said Bent. "I thought she left! Everybody leaves early on Fridays. Even Ms. Cheevy!"

Jordie took a deep breath. She closed her eyes. She opened them again and said, "She's left, all right. Like, *permanently.*"

CHAPTER

12

"Are you sure?" Bent said to Jordie.

Jordie nodded numbly. She was trying to think what to do. But she couldn't think of anything at all.

Polly backed toward the door, her hands to her mouth. "This can't be happening," she said. It wasn't my fault!"

She turned and ran. A moment later her frantic footsteps faded from hearing.

"Shhh!" said Bent. "What's that?"

Heavy footsteps were coming deliberately down the hall.

"Shut the door," gasped Bent.

"Turn out the lights!" Jordie added.

But they were too late. The two of them barely managed, at the last minute, to flatten themselves behind the door.

A huge, heavyset man walked in. He was wearing a shiny suit and a heavy coat with the collar turned up around his thick neck. A hat was pulled low over his fore-head.

He stopped. "Well, well, well," he said. "I thought I'd find you here."

He walked forward again. He stopped. He shook his head. "Pitiful," he said. "Get up and fight like a man."

Bent was about to make a break for it when he heard another set of footsteps. A horrifyingly familiar set.

Dr. Morthouse's.

The heavyset man didn't seem to notice. "You can run but you can't hide, Chalmers," he said. "And rolling over and playing dead won't save you."

Jordie frowned. She took a deep breath, trying to slow down her racing heart.

Dr. Morthouse's authoritative footsteps stopped in the doorway. "What is the meaning of this?" she said in a voice that would freeze mercury.

The heavyset man turned slightly. "Who're you?"

"I'm Dr. Morthouse, principal of Grove Hill Elementary School. And you are?"

"Principal, eh? This one of your teachers?"

There was a long, long pause. Then Dr. Morthouse said, "Has there been some kind of an accident?"

"Oh, I don't think so," said the man. He laughed.

Chills ran down Bent's spine. Jordie shuddered slightly.

A long silence followed as Dr. Morthouse walked over to where Ms. Cheevy lay on the floor. Then, in a flat voice, Dr. Morthouse said, "Ms. Cheevy is dead."

Bent closed his eyes. Jordie stiffened.

The man said, "What? *What?*"

"Did you have anything to do with this?" demanded Dr. Morthouse. She was using the tone that had made more than one student confess and beg for mercy.

"No!" said the man. "Uh, are you sure that she's croaked?" Now he didn't sound so sure of himself.

"What?" said Dr. Morthouse sharply.

"Uh, no, I meant, maybe you're wrong. Maybe we can, uh, do something to save her."

"Unlikely. I don't believe I caught your name?"

"Oh. Right, Doc. I'm, uh, Smith. Bob Smith."

"Well, Mr. Smith, she'd told me she was under a lot of stress and just wanted a nice, quiet teaching job in a small town when I hired her." Dr. Morthouse got up and stood by Mr. Smith. "She mentioned something about doctor's orders. Did you know anything about that?"

"Stress. Yeah, her last job was very high-pressure," said Mr. Smith. "That was it. She had to, uh, sorta retire."

"I see. Of course, I never pried. . . . If you'd care to try artificial respiration?"

"No! I mean, I don't know that mouth-to-mouth stuff."

"If she was a friend of yours, this must be very sad for you, Mr. Smith."

"You're right there." The man seemed to be having difficulty speaking. "We, uh, used to work together before she had to, uh, retire. We'd gotten, like, uh, outta touch, so I'd been looking all over for her. I finally tracked, uh, located her here."

"Oh dear. You have my condolences. What a terrible, terrible shock. You found her like this?"

Jordie and Bent forgot their panic long enough to exchange glances. Dr. Morthouse sounded so warm. So human. But any student at the school would have recognized the insincerity in her voice. It was method number two for inducing confession.

The man didn't confess. He just said, "Yeah. Came through the door and found her stretched out. What a way to go. He's . . ." The man stopped again. "Well, I gotta go."

"Would you like to go to my office and sit down? Have a cup of tea? You've had an awful shock, finding your friend like this. . . . I'll have to call an ambulance, of course. And the police."

"The police? Well, gotta go. Don't worry 'bout me. Bodies don't bother me. I'll, ah, get over it."

"But Mr. Smith!"

"Yeah, gotta go. Business. You know how it is. Can't stay." The heavy footsteps began to retreat toward the door.

"Mr. Smith? Mr. Smith!"

The footsteps sped up. Once he was through the door, Mr. Smith broke into a lumbering run.

Dr. Morthouse knelt back down by Ms. Cheevy.

It was their only chance. "Now," breathed Bent, giving Jordie a nudge. He slid around the door and out of the room. Jordie followed.

In a second they were in the hall, tiptoeing away from the scene of the crime as fast as they could.

Had she seen them? A cold sweat broke out on Bent's forehead. *If we just get out of here alive,* he thought, *I'll never do anything like this again. I'll never even tell another joke.*

"I think we made it," Jordie whispered as they reached the end of the hall. They pushed against a door that wouldn't budge.

Locked. Dead-bolted. Suddenly an icy hand fell on each of them.

"Ahhh!" Jordie howled.

Bent lunged forward.

Dr. Morthouse had a grip of steel.

It was useless to struggle. They were trapped. Caught. They were dead.

"Suppose you tell me what is going on here," said Dr. Morthouse.

"It was an accident," squeaked Bent.

"Yeah. We came back. I forgot my backpack and . . ." Jordie's voice trailed off.

Don't look her in the eye, thought Bent. *You'll confess for sure.*

Jordie stared at Dr. Morthouse helplessly. Then she said, "It was all our fault. We did it! I confess, I confess!"

"You did what, exactly?"

"Found Ms. Cheevy," Bent interrupted in desperation. "We didn't want you to think—"

"Bentley. Look at me."

Bent looked down at his sneakers.

"Bentley."

He looked up into Dr. Morthouse's terrible ice-gray eyes.

"I confess!" he shrieked, his nerve giving way completely. "We did it! We killed Ms. Cheevy."

"But it was an accident," said Jordie. "It was just supposed to be a *joke*! Ms. Cheevy wasn't even supposed to be there. It was supposed to be me."

Still holding each of them, Dr. Morthouse stepped forward and peered out the door. She watched as a large, dark, anonymous-looking car with tinted windows roared out of the parking lot.

Then she nodded. She let go of Jordie and locked the back door of the school. Then she grabbed Jordie again.

"Come with me," she said to Bent and Jordie.

"See, it was a joke," Bent said as Dr. Morthouse marched them down the hall. "Jordie was going to be Ms. Cheevy and Polly thought she was scaring her and then Jordie was going to pretend to be dead—"

"—Only Basement, ah, Mr. Bartholomew almost caught me and I was late and Ms. Cheevy really was still here."

"So Polly scared the real Ms. Cheevy. But we didn't mean to do it. We're sorry. Really. I'll, we'll never, ever do anything like this again. Ever. I promise," said Bent.

Dr. Morthouse steered them into Ms. Cheevy's classroom, where the corpse's legs still stuck out from behind the desk. Bent heard his voice trail off into a Polly-like whimper.

"I'd like to include my assurances that such an incident

will never, ever happen again," said Jordie.

Dr. Morthouse let go of their shoulders and slammed the classroom door shut behind her.

"I wouldn't make promises I couldn't keep," said a hoarse, gravelly voice.

Bent jumped.

Jordie jumped.

Bent turned right.

Jordie turned left.

They crashed into Dr. Morthouse, who was standing between them.

She grabbed them both again and shook them hard.

And the corpse of Ms. Cheevy sat up and leaned forward to look at them from around the edge of the desk.

CHAPTER
13

"Lemme go, lemme go!" screamed Bent.

Jordie put her hands up to cover her eyes.

Ms. Cheevy got up from behind the desk.

Jordie lowered her hands and recovered the use of her voice. "You're not dead!" she gasped.

"Not yet," said Ms. Cheevy.

"Oh, Ms. Cheevy, I am so glad!"

"Are you, Jordie? Somehow, I got the feeling that you didn't think much of my teaching abilities."

Bent said, "Is this some kind of a joke?" He was outraged.

Ms. Cheevy shook her head. "Sorry to put you two through this, but unfortunately, it's not."

"What is going on?" asked Bent. "Why . . ."

His voice trailed off in shock as Ms. Cheevy reached up and took off her hair.

Jordie said, "That's why you wear so much bad

95

makeup. And why your feet are so big. And your clothes are so . . . so . . ."

"Yes. Precisely."

"No way," said Bent. "You're not dead."

"No. And I'm not Ms. Cheevy, as Jordie has now correctly deduced."

"Jordie, Bent, allow me to introduce Mr. Chalmers," Dr. Morthouse said.

"This is a joke, right?" said Bent. "A big, sick joke. You're Ms. Cheevy's twin brother and she's hiding. It's a plan to get back at us for . . ." Bent stopped himself just in time.

To his horror, Dr. Morthouse finished the sentence, "For all your practical jokes. Hardly my method of dealing with infractions, Bent, I think you'll agree."

"It's not a joke?" asked Jordie slowly.

"Nope." Mr. Chalmers sat down on the desk and took off his glasses. He rubbed his eyes. He looked at each of them in turn. "What I'm about to tell you is top secret. It can never be told to another living soul.

"I work for the government as a, well, an information gatherer."

"You're a *spy*?" asked Bent, his jaw dropping.

Mr. Chalmers winced. "It's not a word we use. Let me just say that, as an international freelance photographer, I had a chance to do quite a bit of covert activity as a government operative."

"You *are* a spy!" cried Jordie.

Mr. Chalmers winced again, but he let it go and continued. "About a year ago, my cover was blown. Certain enemies came after me. I barely escaped with my life and I went into hiding. My, um, employers set up a new identity for me in a new place. Since it was done so quickly, this was what they came up with. I was to stay here until the heat died down, then take on another identity and retire someplace nice and warm. And safe."

"Wow," breathed Bent. "This is *excellent*."

"Dr. Morthouse knew, naturally. In fact, it was she who was alerted to the fact that my cover had been blown again when someone called the school, looking for a math teacher. They pretended they represented an employment agency, but she discerned that they were lying."

Jordie and Bent exchanged glances. *Of course.* Who would want to hire Ms. Cheevy / Mr. Chalmers? She—he—was the worst math teacher ever.

"I was always nervous and uncomfortable in my role as a math teacher. I'm afraid it wasn't a very good disguise."

"Fooled me," Bent assured him. Jordan said nothing.

"I became increasingly afraid. I began to look for a way out. I was beginning to panic. And then as I was leaving school this evening I recognized the car of an old, ah, business rival, Mr. Smith, turning into the parking lot. I came back inside and prepared for the worst.

"That was when Polly appeared in her absurd ghost outfit."

"Absurd? Absurd? Do you know how much that cost me?" Bent was outraged again.

"Shhh," said Jordie, pinching his arm.

"I knew that it was only a matter of time before Mr. Smith appeared. When Polly leaped out, I played dead instinctively, trying to buy myself more time."

He looked at the principal.

She said, "I heard someone scream. When I got here, I saw Mr., er, Smith. I realized who he was immediately. When I knelt down beside Mr. Chalmers, I also realized that he wasn't dead and that he of course wished Mr. Smith to think he was. I believe you witnessed the rest."

"Did we ever," said Bent. "Wow. Unbelievable. Awesome!"

"I am truly amazed." Jordie paused. "But what now? What about Polly?"

"That's the best part," said Bent. "She thinks she killed you, Ms., I mean, Mr. Chalmers."

Dr. Morthouse said, "We can't have that."

"Why not?" asked Bent. He met Dr. Morthouse's hard eyes and gave in. "Oh, all right."

Mr. Chalmers said, "Well, this buys me some time."

Dr. Morthouse said, "I'll finish locking up and we'll get you out of here."

He nodded. "Yeah. He'll find out I wasn't dead, of course. But by then I'll be someplace—and someone— that no one will ever guess."

Dr. Morthouse nodded and walked briskly out of the room.

Jordie, Bent, and Mr. Chalmers all looked at one another.

Bent said, "I should've guessed."

"I'm glad you didn't."

"Chicken Cheevy," said Jordie wonderingly, staring at him. "Now I know why you were so nervous all the time—and why you were such a rotten teacher."

Mr. Chalmers shook his head and smiled ruefully. "You know, I was a math teacher, once upon a time. My very first job out of school. But it was brutal. Too much hard work for too little pay. So I got a job I could handle."

"You think being a spy is easier than being a teacher?" asked Bent.

"Infinitely."

Dr. Morthouse walked briskly back into the room. She looked at Bent and Jordie. "You will tell Polly that this was, in fact, a joke. I'm sure you'll be able to convince her."

"No problem," said Bent.

Mr. Chalmers put his wig back on.

"Time to hit the road," he said. "I can't drive my car away from the school, of course."

"Mr. Bartholomew knows a way out that . . . ," Dr. Morthouse began, then realized that Bent and Jordie were still there. She fixed them with her steely gaze. "You two," she said, "get out of here."

"But—" said Bent.

"Now!"

"Right," he said.

"We're going," said Jordie.

They turned and ran.

"She's retired? Just like that?" said Polly. She looked slightly sick. "You mean it really was a joke?"

"The whole thing. It was just a dummy on the floor. Jordie hid behind the desk, then slipped out when you came out into the hall. She came back in just in time to keep you from looking at the dummy too closely."

"Outstanding job," said Park.

"And no more Cheevy, either," said Maria.

Polly repeated dully, "She's not dead. She just, like, retired."

"Dr. Morthouse announced it first thing Monday morning. Too bad you were out sick. You would have found out sooner and you wouldn't have had to worry the whole weekend."

"Why didn't someone call me and tell me?"

No one answered. They all just looked at Polly.

Then Bent said, "Why did you call in sick for three days?"

"Because you thought you'd killed Ms. Cheevy," said Jordie when Polly didn't answer. "You ran off and left us standing there. I suspect, strongly, that you were going to try to make us take the blame."

Polly's cheeks flushed. "I was not. At least, not really."

"I bet you were," said Maria. "I wish I could have seen you run screaming out of the building!"

"I wasn't screaming!"

"She's technically correct," said Jordie. "She was just running."

"Who cares?" said Polly shrilly. "And I knew she wasn't dead all along. I did!" She turned and stomped up the steps.

The door opened.

Dr. Morthouse stood there. "Polly," she said, "feeling better?"

"Yes," Polly said firmly. She edged around Dr. Morthouse and into the school.

Dr. Morthouse stayed in the doorway a moment longer. She looked down at Bent and Jordie.

She didn't smile. She didn't wave. She didn't change expression.

She stepped back and closed the door.

Bent had a sudden, horrible thought.

Was Dr. Morthouse capable of pulling the most elaborate joke of all? What if she and Mr. Chalmers and even Mr. Smith had planned the whole thing?

Nah. It wasn't possible.

Whoever heard of a teacher and a principal conspiring together to practically scare their students to death?

It could never happen. That was one joke that was just too sick to imagine.

Take this pop quiz—and find out if your teacher makes the grade!

1. How does your teacher get to school?
   A. Car
   B. Hearse
   C. Yellow school bus
   D. UFO

2. What color are your teacher's eyes?
   A. Brown
   B. Red
   C. Blue
   D. What eyes?

3. What does your teacher usually eat for lunch?
   A. Tunafish
   B. Monkey brains
   C. Chocolate milk shake, jellybeans
   D. Scrap metal

4. After school, your teacher can be seen:
   A. In the classroom, grading papers
   B. In the graveyard
   C. At the video arcade
   D. Peeling off its skin

5. A typical homework assignment from your teacher is:
   A. Reading a chapter in a textbook
   B. Making a smelly potion

   C. Reading a comic book, cover to cover
   D. Communicating telepathically with life on other planets

6. What is your teacher's favorite sport?
   A. Soccer
   B. Rat racing
   C. Snowboarding
   D. Interplanetary stickball

7. What is your teacher's favorite drink?
   A. Diet cola
   B. Dog-tail tea
   C. Ice cream soda
   D. Sand

Write the number of times you've answered each letter:

A_____
B_____
C_____
D_____

If you've answered mostly

A: Sounds like your teacher is a textbook case of normal!
B: Get out of school as fast as you can! Your teacher is a monster!
C: Are you sure this is your teacher? Cool!
D: Your teacher is an alien!